FULL SERVICE MAID

DIRTY BILLIONAIRE BOSS

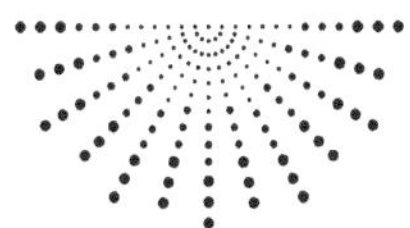

TALA MELTON

GET NAUGHTY UPDATES

Full Service Maid: Dirty Billionaire Boss

 This book contains adult material and scenes of a graphic and adult nature, and some profanity which some may find offensive. All characters are 18 or over.

eISBN: 978-1-62327-808-3

Print ISBN: 978-1-62327-809-0

CHAPTER ONE

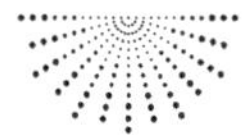

The winter chill had come in quickly this year, billionaire JP Botha taking it in from the third-floor balcony of his Sandhurst mansion. The cup of coffee in his hands passed almost begrudgingly to his lips, not tasting nearly as good as it did in his head. The sudden appearance of another human figure near his massive swimming pool caught him a little, pulling him out of his own head.

"Didn't you leave..." He asked, unintentionally sipping the coffee again.

"No. I'm sorry. I had a problem with my passport!" Candice, his 23-year old housekeeper, stood against the wonderfully leafy view of the plush Johannesburg suburb. She spoke in an almost staccato, something that made the combination of her pale velvety skin and reddish-brown hair seem perfect if she was Columbian. She was not.

"Oh yes, you were supposed to have it renewed..." JP remembered her asking for a day off to this effect.

"Yes, sir... Let me come up," she said, realizing the absurdity of shouting responses to her boss, who also happened to be twice her age.

"Bring me a better cup," JP said, frowning at the cup he was still clutching in his hand.

It took less than 10 minutes for Candice to appear in the doorway of her boss's bedroom, knocking lightly.

"Come through," JP shouted from the balcony, wrapping his dressing-gown tighter around himself. He was still naked underneath it and also sporting a semi-hard on, a side-effect of the hour. He was also exceptionally endowed, so he needed to be quick about finding a way to position himself as inconspicuously as possible.

Almost too quickly, Candice appeared on the terrace, though, forcing the semi-aroused billionaire to turn around and rest his mast against the railings. She placed the coffee on the tiny table on the balcony and poured JP a cup straight from the plunger. She handed it to him at a bit of an angle because he wouldn't face her, something she didn't find strange at all.

"I could make a few calls and get you home if you like..." JP said suddenly, as much to show his power as to be a gentleman. The smell of the coffee made him wish with all that he had that she would say no, though.

"It's alright, sir, don't worry about it. I promise I won't be in your way..." Candice's response was music to his ears.

"Are you sure," he asked, needing to be sure himself.

"I'm sure... Can I make you breakfast..." she asked, not being polite, but because it was her job.

Candice was relieved that her staying seemed to go down well with her boss. She made a mental note to stay out of his way as she cooked him breakfast. She also planned dinner with her eyes on the pantry and fridge. A hearty Italian pasta would be perfect for this winter weather, she thought.

"Breakfast, sir..." She pushed the door open after making her presence behind it known. She walked to the balcony again and put the food down. JP came out of the bathroom wrapped in a towel. Just a towel. She bowed her head to avoid staring at him and started to make an awkward exit.

"Am I eating alone..." JP asked her as he put three crispy strips of bacon in his mouth.

Candice was taken aback. She stopped in the terrace doorway and looked up, questioning him with her eyes. His eyes were on her, too, looking up and down her uniform. She was uncomfortable suddenly and started to straighten her skirt.

"There is nothing wrong with your uniform. It's just unnecessary... it's just the two of us here!"

This statement of fact was incredibly loaded, and Candice caught the double entendre. She fought back a chuckle, searching her head for an appropriately worded response. It wouldn't come, though.

"Go get changed and bring yourself a plate," JP said, giving her an easier-to-follow instruction. She nodded at him and left the room.

When she returned, a fresh plunger of coffee and an extra setting in her hands, she was no less uncomfortable than she had been earlier. She was searching her head again for an appropriate non-offensive way to escape what was shaping up to be an awkward dining experience.

However, awkward it was not!

JP guided the conversation, making it all about the young, beautiful farm girl from Zimbabwe-born to a German father and a South American mother. This explained her exotic appearance, JP thought. He learned, during their casual breakfast, that she had needed a break from her life, and so she decided on a working holiday. The agency had suggested housekeeping in South Africa, which was, according to Candice's research, miles better than working as a nanny in Dubai. And so here she was!

JP gave little of himself away, except for the fact that he

really didn't seem to mind the cold. He sat through the entire encounter wrapped in nothing but a towel to ward off the winter chill, and he seemed remarkably comfortable. As she cleared the plates and made her way downstairs, she couldn't help but notice how incredibly well-built the Afrikaaner giant was. He was also very pleasant to behold.

JP was also thinking of Candice in a way that was inappropriate and also made him look forward to dinner...

CHAPTER TWO

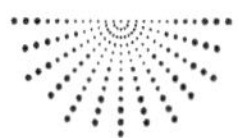

By the time JP had made his way down the stairs, Candice was done cooking.

"Something smells Italian..." JP said as he entered the kitchen.

"Good nose..." Candice said as she went for the serving dish containing the most delicious smelling pasta.

"Let's eat in here," he said, pointing to the breakfast counter. For the second time that day, Candice was taken aback, but she didn't show it this time. She just casually set up dinner on the granite counter.

By the time she was ready and seated, JP had opened a bottle of wine and poured them both a glass. He handed hers to her, and she took it, her fingers shaking. She took a quick sip and hoped that the warm liquid would get her to relax. It didn't, though, and so she just sat down. The discomfort must have been visible on her face.

"Do I make you uncomfortable, " he asked.

"A little..." she said.

"Don't worry; I'm no Christian Grey..." He said,

impressing even himself with this modern-day pop culture reference.

"You've watched 50 Shades," she asked, surprised.

"I read a review somewhere... Not my type of film..."

"Thank goodness," she responded before she could stop herself.

JP was the one who was taken aback now. He looked at her, intrigued. Was this an attempt at humor? Was this natural deflection a part of her character? If it was, he really liked it. He also wondered how far he could push the innuendo with her.

"I do bite, though... but very, very gently..." He was pushing the proverbial envelope now, just a little.

"I don't mind a little bite," she said before silencing herself with a fork full of pasta. JP silenced himself with a huge gulp of wine.

They sat and ate in relative silence for a short while before they both burst into laughter. They knew, of course, why they were laughing, but neither of them called any further attention to it. JP initiated the continued conversation, thankfully keeping it light and easy now. This made the rest of the dinner more comfortable.

He opened another bottle of wine as Candice cleared up. She was loading the dishwasher when he appeared, glass in hand, behind her. She got to her feet and turned into him, taking the glass once she had steadied herself. JPs eyes were lingering on parts of her they shouldn't, and so she tried in vain to shield her beautiful cleavage with the stem and base of the wine glass.

"You can do that tomorrow," JP said, his eyes on where the wraparound white dress covered her thighs. There was no need for him to articulate what was on his mind now and what was quickly being planted in hers. She had vowed to stay professional, but her more and more attractive as the night went on, the boss was making it very difficult.

She tried to slide from his towering gaze, but JP stepped forward and stopped her, pressing her against the side of the counter. Immediately Candice felt the blood rushing to her head and warming the entire length of her body. She couldn't move suddenly, managing only to get the glass in her hand to her lips.

"What happens in quarantine stays in quarantine right," he asked, the lust heavy in his eyes.

"I don't think that's how the saying goes..." Candice was struggling to breathe now. She was hot in places she shouldn't be, but she couldn't help herself. The trickle-down her thighs cooled as it escaped her, and she was shocked by how quickly he had managed to get her aroused. A master at the art of seduction, he clearly was.

"Who cares how it goes? You know what it means, right," JP was coming towards her mouth fast.

"I do," she said, at the exact moment, their lips met.

His mouth on hers was hot. His tongue in her mouth was even hotter. She gripped the stem of the glass harder, scared that she might just drop it and bring this experience to an abrupt end. JP lifted her off the ground and onto the counter without putting his own glass down or removing his lips from hers. He really was incredibly strong.

When he eventually lifted his mouth from hers, she downed the remainder of the wine and put the glass away from her on the counter. She gripped his head and pulled his face back to hers, and now it was her who was kissing him. Quickly, he was kissing her back, relieved mostly that his efforts were not in vain.

His hands moved up and down on her legs, over the dress. He pressed gently into the flesh of her thighs but not so gently as to not send shards of pleasure to her center.

Candice's legs opened involuntarily, and JP slid his fingers underneath her dress. Making direct contact with her flesh now, the heat from his fingers intensified the sensations being sent through her, through all of her now.

Candice undid the drawstring that was keeping her dress in place herself. There was nothing else she could do now to let JP know that she was in complete agreement with what was happening right now. She needed him to know this!

CHAPTER THREE

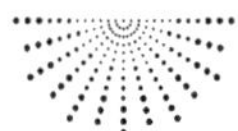

JP pulled the dress away from her skin. He looked down to discover that she had no underwear on. She felt exposed, vulnerable, but all in a very good way. He kissed his thank you onto her lips again as he pulled the dress from her body completely. She kissed him back, deeper, harder.

Then he lifted her off the counter and carried her to where they had just had dinner. With space clear now, he lay her down easily on the cold surface. The contrast created by the air conditioning made this whole experience rather thrilling.

Her flesh raised in delicate bumps now. JP moved his fingertips over the surface, not flattening them, not encouraging them, but simply enjoying them. She watched his fingers move over her for a while but couldn't do this for long. She just closed her eyes and lay back, relaxing into the sensation.

"You are incredibly beautiful," he said.

She couldn't respond, his fingers lingering between her thighs now. He wasn't quite touching her there yet, but the intention was clear, and it was this promise that excited her. He watched her body shake at his touch, and he loved the visual of it.

When he lifted his hands off her, she was shaken from her revelry. She looked up to where he was and found him not there. He was standing against the side of the counter, unbuttoning his shirt. He took it off and then unbuckled his belt. He undid the top button and then pulled down his zip. He paused.

Candice's eyes were on him, on the place his fingers now lingered. She wondered why he was hesitating but didn't ask. There was no way to articulate this question, though, so she knew she would have to wait. But waiting was hard!

There was a lot of time passing between them now, and Candice started to panic deep within. Had he changed his mind, she wondered? Did he suddenly see that this was not a good idea? Her panic was now easily visible on her face.

Then he took off his trousers, along with his underwear. As he struggled, her eyes were on the parts of him that he was trying to hide. He was fully erect now, and his pink hardness was thick and long and looked incredibly dangerous.

When he had taken off his shirt, he stood there and looked at her face. He knew, of course, why she was suddenly nervous. There was nothing that he could say to put her at ease now, but he knew that he was skilled at making her feel that it would be okay. He just needed to be sure that she would give him the opportunity.

"I promise I'll be gentle..."

"Not too gentle... I won't break!"

JP took her legs in his hands and parted them. He pulled her across the surface of the counter until her bottom half was almost over the edge. Her last comment lingered in his head, and he was incredibly excited. But while he appreciated her willingness and bravery, he knew from experience that he would need to get her as warm, wet, and ready as possible.

He started to kiss her from her knees down towards her central place. He grazed over it casually and placed his lips on her opposite thigh. Over and over again, he moved his mouth on the flesh of her legs, gently and deliberately skirting over what had become, for both of them, the most important part of her body.

Then his lips settled on this yearning place. She shuddered almost uncontrollably now. He held down her legs a little harder and pressed his lips against her just a little bit harder. She was dripping a real rainstorm now!

"You taste amazing," JP said without really having tasted her. His tongue was yet to make contact, but the smell of her had already made its way onto his tastebuds, so he felt like he had already taken her onto his tongue.

Then he did, and it was everything he thought it would be. It was so beautiful that he licked the outside of her briefly, before sending his tongue into her and keeping it there. He wasn't moving. Not his tongue, not his face. Her aroma fused beautifully with her taste, and this literally paralyzed him.

Candice needed him to move, though...

She started to move herself against his mouth, but this wasn't satisfying. She really needed JP to snap out of it and get back to the control he was exhibiting just a short while ago. She needed the Alpha he was already proving himself to be.

Candice put her feet on his back and squeezed his head, pulling him deeper into her. She pressed down hard on his mugg so that, eventually, JP did come out of his stupor. And this happened just in the nick of time!

His tongue slipped out of her and then went back in. Again it was out of her briefly before making its way back inside her. This movement put her at ease, and so she relaxed the death grip she had on his head.

He was deathly quiet now. His focus was on what he was doing and nothing else. The same couldn't be said for Candice, though. She was moaning incredibly loudly, her breathing as loud. It was a good thing that they were alone in the house.

JP was licking the external parts of her now. It felt as beautiful as it did when he was inside her, albeit less intense. This was okay, though, she thought, because at least now he was touching her.

CHAPTER FOUR

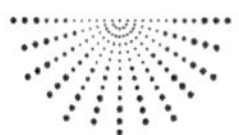

His tongue went deep inside her now and lingered. It didn't stop moving, but it remained inside her. She was close, so close that she had already surrendered in her mind to what she knew would come at any moment now.

When he did leave her, moments before she reached climax, she screamed. Was he teasing her deliberately, she wondered. What was his game plan, if not to get her close and then send her back?

Candice wanted to bring him back into her, but it was too late. He was already standing, pulling her just a little bit more off the counter. He positioned himself between her thighs now and slipped just his head inside her. He stopped and kept a close eye on her face.

She gasped, unintentionally. Yes, her orgasm had been sent running, but there was suddenly this new and bold intention that made her keen with anticipation. She hadn't thought it would be this quickly, but now that it was happening, she knew she wasn't ready.

JP sent two inches plus head into her, and again her gasp

was loud. She couldn't breathe, despite the massive amounts of air being dispelled from her lungs. He pulled these few inches from her and then sent them back into her. Over and over again, he gently fed her just these few inches of himself, all the while watching her face closely.

Then she turned to him and opened her eyes. Their gaze locked, and JP entered her with two more inches. Again she gasped, but quickly her gasp became a loud moan. With just these five or six inches, he was once again steadying her towards orgasm.

"You feel..." he started saying but couldn't complete his sentence. Candice writhed from side to side underneath him, clearly caught in the throes of orgasm.

"Amazing..." she whispered over and over again, more to the response of what was happening between her legs. She lifted her head to see, to gain visual confirmation of what was going on. She could hold herself up briefly, just enough for her to see that there was more of him outside her than was in.

He, too, was looking at the entry he had gained. He was also mesmerized by the coating from her depths all over his shaft. This excited him, but it also entranced him so that he fed her two more easy inches of himself. He was careful not to go too deep, though, so as not to interrupt her climax.

It took the longest minute for her to reach a complete climax. She went in and out of her own daze while JP returned to his razor-sharp focus. He needed to concentrate now in order to make this experience as beautiful for her as he could, in the hope that when it was his turn, she would remember and reciprocate.

Candice arched her back and closed her eyes again. The whole room was dark once more, reduced to the sensation between her thighs. JP gripped her legs hard to steady her on the descent. Then, at the perfect time, he fed her a couple more inches of himself.

He went in deliberately slowly. Everything inside him wanted to send the full length of his shaft into her, but he kept reminding himself that slow and steady won the race. He eased a few more inches into her until he had passed the halfway mark. Then he paused.

As slowly he began to pull himself out of her. And then, with as much care, he drove himself back into her. He was thrusting, but he also wasn't. He was just stretching her out as gently and carefully as he could.

He wanted to fill the silence with words, but the look on her face said that he shouldn't, and so he didn't. He just kept a firm hold of her legs and moved in and out of her with half of his hardness. The feeling was intense, but Candice was taking it, managing quite well more than he ever hoped she would.

"Deeper," she whispered suddenly, exciting the already overstimulated man. He didn't dare, for the moment at least. Using every reserve of self-control that he had, he just eased her wider and wider, making her just that little bit more receptive to more of himself without giving her this more.

Two-thirds of his massive length was inside her when he realized that she wouldn't be able to take anymore. This realization settled over him like an achievement. He had tested her limits and found out how far she would stretch. This was all the information he needed. With this length, he thrust into her a little harder, extracting himself almost completely from her and then pushing just this part of himself back inside her.

They were again both deathly quiet. It wasn't an uncomfortable silence, though, so he felt no need to try and fill the space with words. Her moaning was getting louder, though, so that he knew that she was again close, so he knew that all he needed to do was maintain his military momentum.

He did, and again she was climaxing. She was cumming harder than she had before, and this again excited him. He tried, unintentionally, for more, but her crevice would yield no more, not yet anyway. All it did was spray even more of her liquid center into the outside world.

"Incredible..." he grunted, without ceasing his thrusting. She felt so good that he too was now close, wondering if he shouldn't perhaps let himself go. He was debating this with a seriousness that came from his acute awareness of self. He knew that once he had cum, that would be it.

With all his strength, he stopped moving and just let her use his erection to finish herself off. He used this time to figure out what would make up the grand finale, what would be his coup de gras. He needed to finish her off as spectacularly as he had started her and also in such a way that would leave him too feeling satisfied...

CHAPTER FIVE

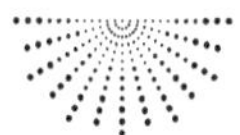

JP lifted Candice off the counter, himself still inside her. He kept her on himself as he swopped them out so that he was now on the counter, half sitting, half lying down. He was careful not to go any deeper into her than she had already let him go. He eased himself onto the counter and up against the wall, his hands gripping her hard at the hips so as to stop himself from impaling her.

She looked at him now, her eyes open. She was shaking, nervous about what he was trying, unsure of what this actually was. When he had positioned himself comfortably, he moved her up and down on himself for a moment, very, very carefully. Only when her knees were on the counter on either side of him did he let her go, knowing that she was now in control of how deep and how hard.

Candice was now moving herself on him. She tried, rather valiantly, for more, but it soon became obvious to her too that what was already inside her was all that was going to get inside her. This settled over her in waves, waves of security and comfort, knowing that they both now knew what they had to work with.

She moved herself up and down on the menacing erection that felt intense and intrusive. It also felt like everything she had wanted for a while now, even though she had never thought that it would come from JP. She pushed hard on him and then pulled as hard away, careful that his head didn't slip from her. It just felt too damn good to have him, any part of him, inside her.

Then she moved in circles. The circles were not wide, but they were definite. JP now closed his eyes, needing to escape into the blackness of his own orgasm. The pit he was about to descend into was deep and dark, yes, but it was very welcome. He had given her full control of his climax now, and he trusted that she would guide him to heaven and back with as much skill as he had done with her.

He felt as Candice kept her circles tight that he was building toward a steady orgasm. He hadn't expected to feel this so soon, but now that he knew it was definitely coming, he lay down on his back completely now. As he positioned himself underneath her, he just trusted that she would hold her own position on top of him.

She did this expertly...

His hands found her breasts, and he pressed hard into the flesh. He wanted to move her hips on him but thought better of it, not wanting to rob her of the pleasure of giving him pleasure. Also, Candice seemed to know exactly what she was doing, and so it was probably best to leave her to it.

"Wow," is all he managed when she was again moving up and down on him, having abandoned the gentle and not so gentle circles of her movements of earlier. There wasn't much more that she could do, but no more was necessary.

Candice was so wet between her thighs now that she really thought that more of JP was inside her. She had convinced herself that all of him was, in fact, inside her now. Her eyes went to the place where their bodies fused, and to her surprise, no more or less of him was inside her. She almost felt disappointed in herself.

JP ran his fingers down her back now and held on to her hips. He could see in her eyes, on her face, that there was a feeling that she was somehow inadequate. He squeezed her hips but didn't push or pull her. He made no effort to gain more entry into her. He simply just held her in place and moved himself up and down as far as the counter would allow.

Then he let her hips go and put his hands underneath his head. He closed his eyes again and relaxed into the control that he had just given back to Candice. She was again moving up and down, again moving in circles. She knew that the limits she faced now presented her with an opportunity. She could take it and do her best with it, or she could give up and let JP get himself over.

The latter was not an option!

She placed her hands on his chest now and took a deep breath. She pressed down hard with all her strength, and just a further two inches slipped into her. This was really all there was going to be as far the entry into her was concerned. JP appreciated the feeling, and he smiled. Then as she started to move in ever-widening circles, he knew that she had surrendered herself to her own ability and that she was about to give the performance of her life.

And perform she did. She pulled his erection in every direction with a skill that she never knew she had. She pushed hard into the massive beasts body and pulled as far away as her short legs could carry her. Over and over again, she moved in complete circles until it was her who was cumming, again. She had hoped that she would bring him to an orgasm, but she had failed. And this failure, like the absolute pleasure of her own orgasm, washed over her face.

Candice fell on JPs chest, and she was spent. He was still

inside her, but she was not moving. She couldn't move. JP let her rest a minute and catch her breath. He didn't move for a moment and just enjoyed the feeling of being inside her.

Slowly he moved her off him and carried her up in his arms. He lay her down on the sofa just off the kitchen. He winked at her and smiled, leaving her to gather herself as he went to pour them more wine.

They drank the wine and chatted about something neither of them could remember as JP inserted just a single finger into her. Then he inserted a second finger and then a third. Her glass almost fell from her hand, and JP caught it in time; such was his focus. He moved his three fingers around in her as she lay back on the couch. Then JP mounted her.

He needed to cum. He wanted to cum. But he also wanted to be sure that she was still okay with letting him cum...

She was, of course.

He thrust into her with a new determination. It was the kind of selfish determination that forced her to surrender, body and mind. She knew she couldn't possibly cum again, but she also knew that the skill of the man moving in her and on her meant that they would both be having an orgasm soon.

And this is exactly what happened. It wasn't even surprising for her; she expected it. It was not surprising for him because he took back the control needed. There was something deeply satisfying about this climax, and JP couldn't move for a long time. Candice wasn't going anywhere either, and so they just lay on the exaggerated sofa and languished in the silence...

"What happens in quarantine stays in quarantine..." Candice whispered just before she fell asleep!

ABOUT THE AUTHOR

Tala Melton is an emerging erotica author of naughty maids and their billionaire bosses.

Readers: I want to expand a few of the stories to see where the characters can be explored further. If there are any of the stories that you would like to read more about again, I'd love to hear from you!

Visit my blog at Tala Melton Blog
Join my newsletter for free exclusive previews Tala Melton Newsletter
Follow me on Twitter at Tala Melton Twitter
Like my page on Facebook at Tala Melton FB

Sign up for Free Stories from Xplicit Press Authors
Xplicit Press Updates
Like Xplicit Press on Facebook
Follow Xplicit Press on Twitter

MORE NAUGHTY MAID STORIES BY TALA MELTON

Naughy Maids and The Dirty Billionaire Bosses

www.ingramcontent.com/pod-product-compliance
Lightning Source LLC
LaVergne TN
LVHW050612100826
845148LV00015B/3232

* 9 7 8 1 6 2 3 2 7 8 0 9 0 *